TWISTERS
RHYMERS

Old Joe Rowan

Christine Moorcroft and
Élisabeth Eudes-Pascal

Evans

Old Joe Rowan lives alone
in a home made of stone.

"I am not on my own," says Joe. "Close by are a goat, a stoat, a sparrow and a foal.

There's a crow and a toad
and a vole. And below the roses
there's a mole in a hole."

When the snow falls
and the wind blows cold,
Joe dozes on his sofa.
The coals in the stove
glow red and gold.

"Oh," thinks Joe.
"Those animals will be cold.
They don't like the snow,
I'm told."

He puts on his coat,
and throws a scarf
around his throat.

Out he goes into the snow.

Are the goat,
    the stoat,
      the foal,
        the sparrow
          and the crow
            all frozen?

No!
They are cosy
and dozing
with the toad and the vole
and the mole in his hole.

Joe's toes,
his nose
and even his bones
are frozen.
"I am so cold,"
he moans.

Nosy Joan Bold
strolls over the road.

She pokes old Joe
with her bony elbow
and says, "Oh, hello."

"Come in from the cold.
I have rolled some dough
at home for a loaf,
to go with a bowl of soap –
no, soup.

27

I try not to boast
but my soup
is better than most."

So off Joe goes
to Joan's cosy home.
Soon, he's warm as toast.

Twisters Rhymers follow on from the success of the **Twisters** series. Twisters are gripping short stories from different genres, told in just 50 words, with an appealing choice of illustration styles and content. Why not try one?